Scan the QR code to read and listen to the glossary words for FREE!

glossary - *Meanings of words.*

Dados Internacionais de Catalogação na Publicação (CIP) de acordo com ISBD

C714a Collodi, Carlo

The adventures of Pinocchio - Easier Classics Reading / Carlo Collodi. – Jandira : W. Books, 2025.

144 p. ; 12,8cm x 19,8cm. – (Easier Classics Reading Library Children's Collection)

ISBN: 978-65-5294-160-2

1. Literatura infantojuvenil. 2. Literatura Infantil. 3. Clássicos. 4. Aventura. 5. Imaginação. 6. Fantasia. I. Título. II. Série.

2025-607

CDD 028.5
CDU 82-93

Elaborado por Vagner Rodolfo da Silva - CRB-8/9410
Índice para catálogo sistemático:
1. Literatura infantojuvenil 028.5
2. Literatura infantojuvenil 82-93

Easier Classics
The Adventures of Pinocchio

Original story by Carlo Collodi.
Text based on the adaptation by Gemma Barder.
Illustrations by Archina Laezza.

1st edition in 2025
www.cirandacultural.com.br

THE ADVENTURES OF PINOCCHIO

Carlo Collodi

W. Books

Meet the Characters

Pinocchio

Geppetto

Cricket

The Blue Fairy

Mangiafuoco

Alfonso

Chapter 1

Geppetto was a **clockmaker** who lived in a small town in Italy. He made beautiful **cuckoo clocks**, and lots of people travelled very far to buy them.

Although everyone loved Geppetto, he was lonely. He wanted a child more than anything else in the world.

clockmaker - *Someone who makes clocks for their job.*

cuckoo clocks - *Clocks that make bird noises every hour as a wooden bird pops out of the clock.*

One night, Geppetto **wished upon a star**. A blue fairy heard Geppetto's wish and gave him a magical block of wood.

The wood didn't look magical. But when Geppetto started working with the block of wood, he could feel the magic inside of it.

wished upon a star - When someone makes a wish when they see a star at night-time.

Geppetto **carved** a little wooden body, arms and legs. Then, he joined everything together with bits of wire.

Once Geppetto had put the little body together, it started to run around the workshop, even though it didn't have a head to see where it was going!

carved - When someone makes something out of wood by cutting it or changing its shape.

Geppetto quickly carved a head, caught the **puppet** and stuck the head on top of its body.

Finally, he painted a face, dungarees and shoes on to the **puppet**.

puppet - A toy of a person or animal which can be moved by a hand inside it or by strings tied to it.

'I will name you Pinocchio,' said Geppetto.

'I like that name!' said Pinocchio.

Geppetto was shocked. He knew the wood was magic, but didn't realise the magic was so strong!

Not only could Pinocchio move without any strings, but he could talk too!

'You can talk?' asked Geppetto.

'Of course I can talk, **Papa**!' said Pinocchio, smiling.

Geppetto smiled back. He was so happy! No one had ever called him '**papa**' before.

Papa - *Another name for a dad or father.*

Chapter 2

Before Geppetto carved him into a puppet, Pinocchio was just a piece of wood that couldn't move or walk around.

This meant Pinocchio only knew what Geppetto taught him.

So Geppetto tried to teach Pinocchio everything he thought a young boy should know.

Geppetto loved Pinocchio,

but Geppetto was frightened.

He thought that people would be scared of a puppet that could walk and talk without strings.

He was worried they might hurt Pinocchio. Geppetto decided to keep Pinocchio inside so he would be safe.

'Why can't I go outside?' asked Pinocchio.

'Sometimes people are afraid of things that are new or different,' said Geppetto. 'They might be scared of you and hurt you.'

'That sounds very silly,' said Pinocchio.

'It does, doesn't it?' Geppetto laughed. 'But you must stay inside where you are safe.'

Pinocchio quickly became bored of living in Geppetto's workshop.

He hid Geppetto's tools and ran away from him when Geppetto tried to get them back.

Even without strings, Pinocchio could run very fast. Much faster than the old clockmaker! This was fun for Pinocchio, but not very fun for Geppetto, who got tired very quickly.

One evening, when Geppetto had gone to sleep, Pinocchio sat next to the **fireplace**.

'Excuse me, young man,' said a voice.

Pinocchio looked around but couldn't see anyone.

'Down here!' said the voice.

fireplace - *The place in a house where you put a fire.*

When Pinocchio looked down, he saw a green cricket sitting next to him.

'Who are you?' asked Pinocchio.

'I'm your friend,' said Cricket. 'I will help you to learn what is right and wrong. The Blue Fairy sent me to help you.'

Chapter 3

One day, Pinocchio asked Geppetto if he could go to school.

'Why do you want to go to school?' asked Geppetto.

'I want to learn things and meet real children,' said Pinocchio.

Pinocchio had behaved much better since meeting Cricket. He hoped Geppetto would trust him now.

The next morning, Pinocchio came downstairs and found books, new pencils and a red apple on the table.

'Are these for school, Papa?' asked Pinocchio, happily.

'They are, my son,' said Geppetto. 'I have spoken to the **headmaster**, and I have told the school everything about you. They said that you can start this morning!'

headmaster - The person who is in charge of a school.

Pinocchio went upstairs to get ready. Cricket jumped on to his shoulder.

'How did Papa pay for the books, the pencil and the apple?' asked Pinocchio.

'He sold his good coat,' said Cricket. 'So, you must be very good and work hard in school to show him how thankful you are.'

Pinocchio had a great day at school. The boys and girls were excited to have a boy made out of wood in their class, and the teacher was very kind to Pinocchio.

But Pinocchio was worried.

He kept thinking that when winter came, Geppetto would be too cold without his good coat.

As Pinocchio walked home, a tall man with a thin, black **moustache appeared**.

'A puppet that moves without strings!' said the man. 'You could be the **star of my show**!'

'No, thank you,' replied Pinocchio. 'I am going home to my papa.'

'But I could pay you!' said the man.

moustache - *The hair that grows above someone's lips and below their nose.*

appeared - *When something is seen that wasn't there before.*

star of my show - *The most important person in a show.*

Chapter 4

The man's name was Mangiafuoco. He held out a bag of gold coins.

'Perform in my puppet show tonight and I will give you this bag of coins. I *promise*,' said Mangiafuoco.

Pinocchio wanted the money so he could buy Geppetto lots of coats to keep him warm all winter.

So, Pinocchio went with Mangiafuoco to his puppet show.

'Here you will perform with all of my puppets!' said Mangiafuoco.

When Pinocchio walked past the red curtain and out onto the stage, he realised the theatre was very big.

Pinocchio started to feel very **nervous**.

'I don't think I can perform, Mr Mangiafuoco,' said Pinocchio.

'Don't you want to dance with Alfonso?' said Mangiafuoco, holding a puppet in a green soldier's **suit**.

Alfonso was a beautiful puppet. Seeing him made Pinocchio want to dance with him. So, he did.

nervous - When someone feels scared or worried.

suit - The clothes that someone wears to an important event.

The theatre quickly filled up with children and their parents, waiting for the show to begin.

Music started to play and Mangiafuoco moved the puppets on to the stage. It looked like they were dancing. Everyone cheered!

But when Pinocchio started to dance, everyone cheered and clapped for him far louder than before.

After the show, Pinocchio asked Mangiafuoco for the bag of gold coins.

'I can't let you leave,' said Mangiafuoco. 'I have just sold tickets to people who want to see you in tomorrow's show.'

Then, Mangiafuoco grabbed Pinocchio and quickly locked him away.

PUPPET SHOW
PUPPET SHOW

Chapter 5

Pinocchio was locked away for many weeks.

He had to perform over and over again, travelling to different towns. He never got any money, and he was locked away every night so he couldn't go home to Geppetto.

Every night, Pinocchio looked up at the stars and thought about how much he missed his papa.

Pinocchio was very tired from performing so much.

He was so tired that, during one of the shows, Pinocchio's leg got stuck in Alfonso's strings.

Pinocchio tried to free himself, but became **tangled** and fell on to the stage with Alfonso.

The people watching **booed** and started to leave.

tangled - When something is twisted together until it is messy and tied up.

booed - When people watching a show don't like it and say 'boo'.

Mangiafuoco was very angry.
He **threatened** to chop Alfonso up.

As he picked up his axe, Pinocchio crouched over Alfonso to **protect** him.

'No! I can't let you hurt him,' said Pinocchio. 'He's my only friend.'

threatened - When someone says they are going to hurt someone else.

protect - To look after.

Mangiafuoco was shocked.
He slowly dropped his axe and stared at Pinocchio.

He didn't believe that Pinocchio could feel emotions like a human. He thought Pinocchio was just a puppet made of wood.

But when Mangiafuoco looked at Pinocchio's sad face, he realised he was wrong.

Mangiafuoco looked at Pinocchio and said, 'I'm sorry that I didn't treat you like a real boy.'

'So, you won't chop Alfonso up?' asked Pinocchio.

'No, I promise to never chop Alfonso up,' said Mangiafuoco, putting five gold coins into Pinocchio's hand. 'Now, take these and go.'

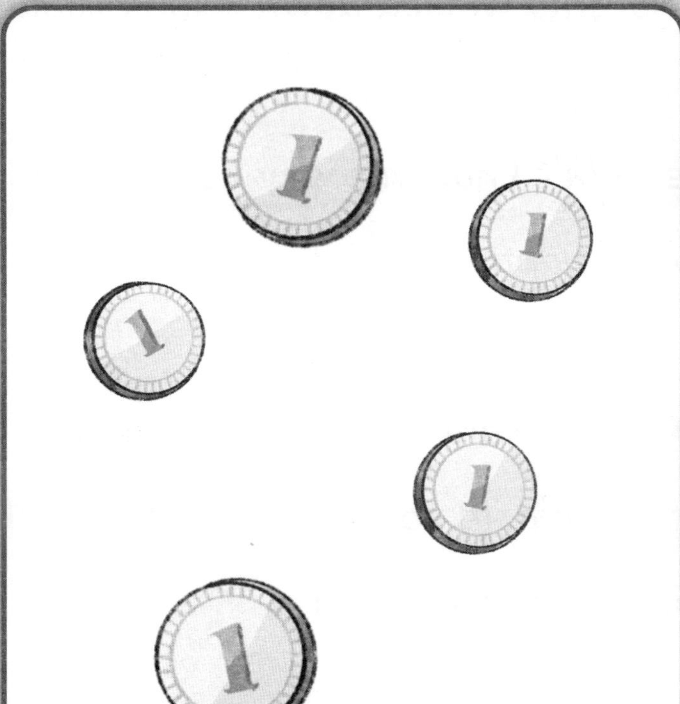

Chapter 6

Pinocchio walked down a long road.

He didn't know his way home back to his papa, Geppetto.

After so many weeks away, he only had five gold coins. It wasn't enough to buy Papa his coat.

He was worried about what Papa would think.

Pinocchio saw a fox and a cat walking side-by-side along the road.

As Pinocchio walked, the coins Mangiafuoco had given him jingled in his hand.

Fox heard and asked, 'What do you have in your hand?'

'Five gold coins,' said Pinocchio. 'It's not enough to buy a new coat for my papa, though.'

Fox grinned and said, 'If you **bury** your gold coins under that **oak tree**, the next day it will grow gold coins.'

'Thank you,' said Pinocchio. 'You are very kind to tell me about that.'

After they had left, Pinocchio ran to the tree. He dug a hole under the big **oak tree** and put the coins into the ground. He covered them with dirt.

Then, he fell asleep.

bury - Put something in the ground.

oak tree - A large tree that grows acorns. (Acorns are fruits that grow on oak trees and have oak tree seeds inside.)

Chapter 7

The next morning, Pinocchio woke up and ran towards the tree.

He searched all over the oak tree to find any coins growing from its branches. But there were no coins.

Pinocchio didn't understand what he'd done wrong.

Suddenly, Pinocchio heard a familiar voice.

It was Cricket!

'Pinocchio! I have been looking for you for many weeks!' said Cricket.

Suddenly - *Quickly and not expected to happen.*

Pinocchio wanted to tell Cricket everything that had happened. But he felt **ashamed**.

So, he lied and said, 'I was taken by a witch! She put a spell on me and there was nothing I could do!'

As he said this, his wooden nose grew three times longer.

ashamed - When someone feels bad about something they have done.

Cricket jumped on to Pinocchio's long nose.

'Is that what really happened?' asked Cricket.

'Yes!' replied Pinocchio, making his nose grow even longer.

'Why is my nose growing?' asked Pinocchio, who looked very worried.

'You are made of magic wood,' said Cricket. 'Every time you lie, your nose will grow. It is better to tell me the truth, Pinocchio.'

Pinocchio told the Cricket about Mangiafuoco, the fox, the cat and about burying his gold coins.

As he told the truth, his nose went back to its normal size.

'Did you ever think the fox and the cat might have lied to you?' asked Cricket. 'Look over there.'

Pinocchio looked at the place where he had buried his gold coins and saw an empty hole.

'The fox and the cat took my coins when I was asleep!' said Pinocchio.

Pinocchio had learnt that he should never trust people he didn't know.

'I want to see Papa,' said Pinocchio.

'Geppetto went away to look for you,' said Cricket. 'He took a boat, and now he's lost at sea.'

Cricket and Pinocchio decided to look for Geppetto by the sea. But no one had seen Geppetto, and there were no boats left.

Then, they saw an old lady struggling to carry her shopping. Pinocchio was worried about trusting strangers. But he knew if he was careful, he would be okay.

Pinocchio ran to the old lady and asked if she needed help.

'You are very kind,' said the old lady. 'Kindness should always be **rewarded**.'

Suddenly, the old lady **transformed** into the Blue Fairy.

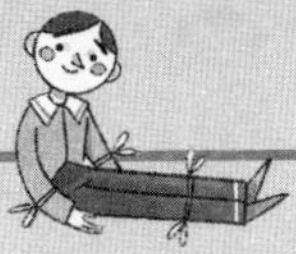

rewarded - When someone is given money or something nice when they have done a good thing.

transformed - Changed into.

Chapter 8

Pinocchio knew that the Blue Fairy had given Geppetto the magic wood that he was made from.

Pinocchio trusted her and asked if she could help them find Geppetto.

'To have a wish **granted**, you must be a good person,' said the Blue Fairy.

granted - Given.

Pinocchio wanted to show the Blue Fairy that he was just as good as his papa.

He went to live with her to show how good he was.

Pinocchio went to school and worked hard. He knew his papa would be **proud** of him.

proud - *The way someone feels when they are happy with their choices or someone else's choices.*

One day, Pinocchio heard that the **carriage** to the Land of Toys was coming to town.

The Land of Toys was a magical island with toys, sweets and fairground rides.

Pinocchio wanted to have fun after being good for so long. He knew he should tell the Blue Fairy where he was going, but he climbed into the **carriage** anyway.

carriage - *An old-fashioned vehicle, usually for a small number of people, which is pulled by horses.*

Chapter 9

Lots of children climbed into the carriage with Pinocchio.

The carriage had no doors or windows, so they couldn't see where they were going. But, they were still excited.

They travelled for what felt like a long time. The carriage began to move side to side. Pinocchio guessed they had now left land and were sailing across the sea.

When the carriage opened its doors, they were all amazed.

They had made it to the Land of Toys; a large, magical island!

It was filled with fairground rides, candyfloss and bright colourful lights. Pinocchio wanted to go on all the rides and eat all the sweets!

After hours and hours of going on fairground rides and eating lots of sweets, Pinocchio was starting to feel ill.

He wanted to go home.
So, he started to look for a way to get off the island.

Soon, he saw a line of children waiting to get on to a boat that would take them off the island.

When Pinocchio joined the line of children, they all looked ill and tired.

But then, he saw the boy standing next to him had grown fluffy donkey ears!

The same thing was happening to Pinocchio! He had donkey ears and a tail!

The Land of Toys wasn't magical or fun.

All the children who came to the Land of Toys became *donkeys*!

As Pinocchio realised this, he changed completely into a donkey too.

Pinocchio started to **gallop** away on his **hooves**, but a group of men stood in his way.

'Quick, grab him!' shouted a man. 'We can't sell the donkeys if they escape into the sea!'

Pinocchio jumped off of the island and started to swim until the island was far away.

gallop - When a horse or donkey runs as fast as it can.

hooves - The hard part on the bottom of the feet of animals such as donkeys, sheep and deer.

Pinocchio tried to call for help, but all he could say was '*hee-haw*'.

If only he could find the Blue Fairy. He needed a wish or else he would drown!

He thought of all the good things that he had done for the Blue Fairy and wished for her help.

Chapter 10

A bright blue light suddenly appeared.

Pinocchio was no longer a donkey.

He had his wooden body again!

He looked around but could not

see the Blue Fairy.

He was alone, **floating** in the sea.

floating - *To stay on the top of water without sinking.*

Pinocchio saw a huge fish swim below him, deep in the ocean. Pinocchio didn't know what the fish would do so he stayed very still.

Suddenly, the huge fish opened its mouth. It had the biggest teeth Pinocchio had ever seen!

Then, it swallowed Pinocchio whole!

Everything was dark and cold.

But Pinocchio was still alive!

He didn't know where he was, but it looked like he was in a big cave.

When Pinocchio looked at the walls, it looked like they were moving.

'H-h-hello?' shouted Pinocchio. 'Is anybody there?'

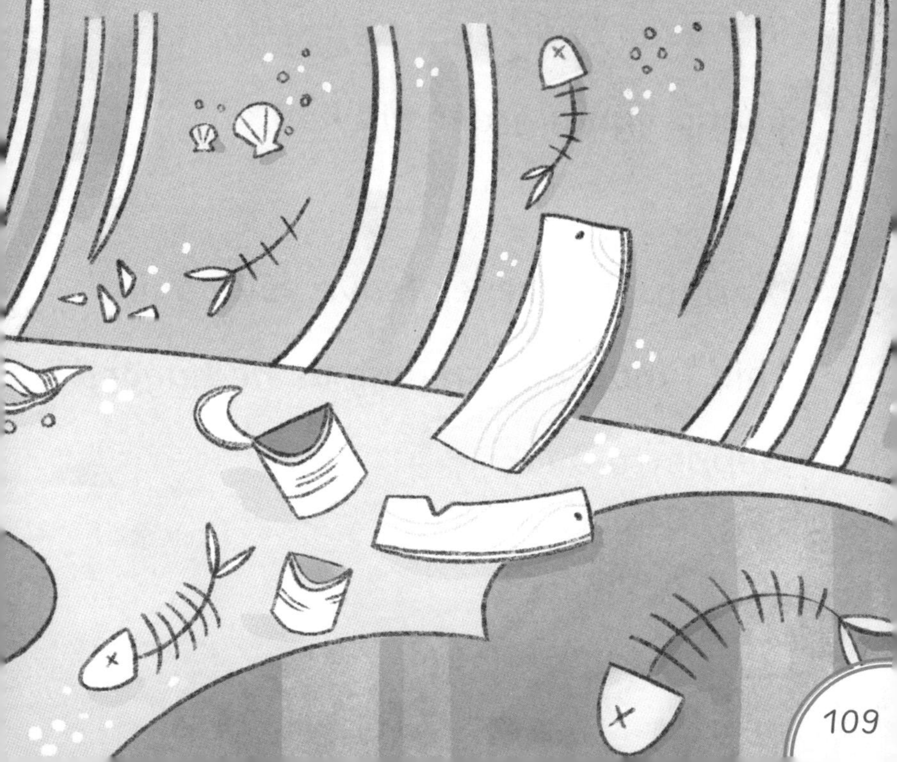

A familiar voice replied,
'P-P-Pinocchio? Is that you?'

Pinocchio ran to the voice.
It was his papa!

'My dear boy!' said Geppetto,
giving him a great big hug.

'Papa! I will never leave you again!'
said Pinocchio, smiling as he hugged
Geppetto back.

Chapter 11

'Where are we, Papa?' asked Pinocchio.

'My son, we are in the belly of a huge shark!' said Geppetto.

Geppetto said that he had been looking for Pinocchio everywhere. When looking for Pinocchio at sea, he was eaten by the huge shark and had been trapped inside for a very long time.

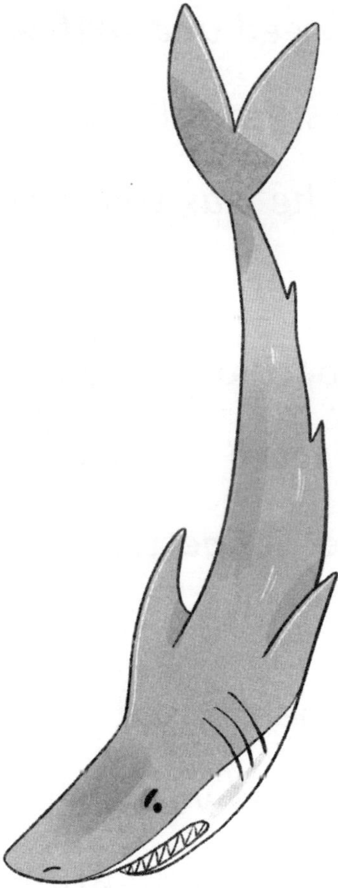

Geppetto wanted to use shells, seaweed and **driftwood** trapped in the shark's belly to make a boat. But he was too tired to collect them.

Pinocchio wanted to help. So he collected the **driftwood** and gave it to Geppetto.

Geppetto used the shells to carve the **driftwood**. Then he tied it with the seaweed until it became a boat.

driftwood - Wood that is found in the sea and floats on to land.

Finally, Pinocchio found two more big pieces of driftwood, and Geppetto carved them into **oars**.

But Geppetto didn't know how to get the boat out of the shark.

'I know a way we can escape,' said Pinocchio, smiling. 'We must wait until night-time.'

oars - Wooden sticks used to move a boat across water.

Chapter 12

Before, when Pinocchio had been collecting the wood for Geppetto, he had realised something.

The shark opened its mouth while it slept during the night. It opened wide enough for them to escape!

They waited for it to become night-time. Quietly, they pushed the boat towards the shark's mouth and waited for it to open wide.

Once the mouth was wide enough, they got into the boat and **rowed** as fast as they could.

They were free!

They danced and cheered in the little boat.

Together, they **rowed** until they found land.

rowed - *To move a boat with wooden sticks called oars.*

Not long after getting back on land, Geppetto became ill and tired because he had spent so long in the shark's cold stomach.

But some kind people found Pinocchio and Geppetto and gave them a place to stay.

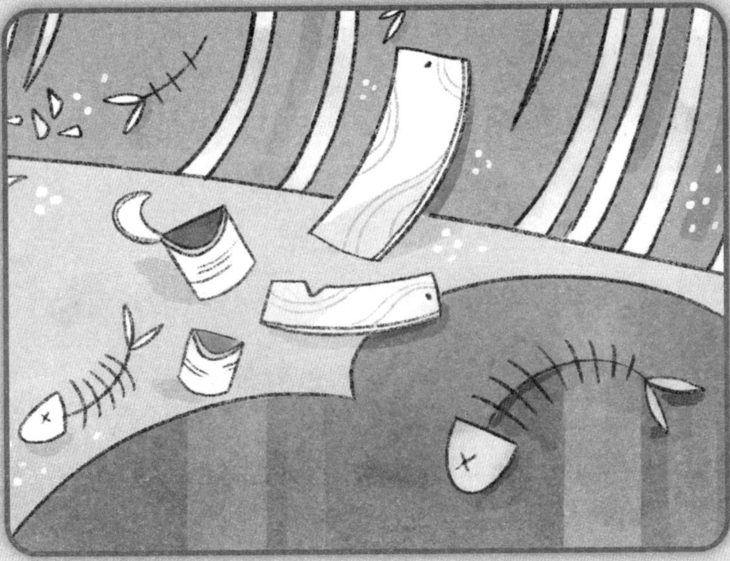

Pinocchio wanted to **repay** the kind people for all their help, so he worked for them every day.

They gave him gold coins in return.

Soon, Pinocchio had enough money to buy a cottage for both him and Geppetto to live in.

repay - *To pay money back or to do something for someone as a thank you for their help.*

One day, Pinocchio heard the **townspeople** talking about a sick old lady.

'I've heard she's the Blue Fairy,' said a man. 'She's very ill, but she can't pay for a doctor.'

Pinocchio asked the man which hospital the sick lady was in.

townspeople - *People who live in a town.*

That evening, Pinocchio counted all the money that he and Geppetto had saved.

He wanted to give all the money straight to the Blue Fairy, but he didn't.

He knew the right thing to do was to tell his papa and ask what to do.

Pinocchio knew that the Blue Fairy had helped them both a lot.

'Papa, I would like to give the Blue Fairy all of our money to help her,' said Pinocchio. 'But only if you want to as well.'

Geppetto was very proud of Pinocchio and said, 'Of course, my son. That is a lovely idea.'

Chapter 13

The next day, Pinocchio and Geppetto found the Blue Fairy in the hospital.

Pinocchio told her everything that had happened to him.

'I'm very sorry for making bad choices in the past,' said Pinocchio. 'But my papa and I are going to pay for your **doctor's bill** and help you until you're better.'

doctor's bill - A list of all the things that someone has to pay for when they get help in a hospital or from a doctor.

Pinocchio visited the Blue Fairy every day.

He brought her flowers from their garden and cakes from the bakery when he could afford it.

The Blue Fairy was happy to see Pinocchio, but she was old and tired. The doctors said that she was too tired to ever get better again.

One day, the Blue Fairy closed her eyes for the last time.

There was a bright blue light, and she **disappeared**.

All that was left of her were blue sparkles in the bed where she had been lying.

disappeared - No longer able to be seen.

Pinocchio walked away to the window. He looked at his reflection and saw that he wasn't wooden.

He was a real boy at last!

He rushed home to Geppetto, but their cottage wasn't there.

Instead, there was a big, beautiful brick house!

Geppetto stepped outside and called, 'Pinocchio, is that you?'

'Yes, Papa. I'm a real boy!' said Pinocchio. 'What happened to our cottage?'

Geppetto told Pinocchio that there was a bright blue light and their cottage changed to the big house.

The Blue Fairy's final wish was to make their dreams come true. After everything they had been through, they were together and happy.

The End.

Carlo Collodi

Carlo Collodi was born in Florence, Italy in 1826.

Collodi worked for a newspaper before he wrote *Pinocchio*.

Collodi wrote many books about Pinocchio which turned into the series *The Adventures of Pinocchio* published in 1883.

It was also made into a Disney film!